Facing My Music

Written by Barbara Seiger

Illustrated by Lisa Papp

STECK-VAUGHN
A Harcourt Company

www.steck-vaughn.com

Contents

CHAPTER 1

*J*itters

Daniel Muldoon rolled onto his back and looked up at the ceiling. Then he checked the clock again. It was almost two in the morning, and he hadn't gone to sleep yet. He sat up in bed and looked out his bedroom window at the full moon that lit up the night. *I'll never get to sleep,* he thought. *And then besides everything else tomorrow, I'll be exhausted.*

Daniel lay back down and pulled his quilt over his head. Going without sleep was bad, but it was "everything else" that was really bothering him. Tomorrow was the last rehearsal before the spring concert. *If I'm this nervous before the rehearsal, what's going to happen at the concert?* He shut his eyes. *I can play that music perfectly,* he told himself. *So why is it that every time I have to play in front of an audience, I can't? Why do my hands shake? Why do I start to sweat? Why is it that every single note floats right out of my head?*

Daniel had been asking those questions for a long time. No one had ever given him a helpful answer—not his music teacher, his mother, his father, or even his grandfather. He had been surprised that his grandfather couldn't help him. After all, his grandfather was a famous pianist and knew all about stage fright. But he always told Daniel the same thing: "Lots of musicians get stage fright. Most of them get over it eventually."

Daniel always asked his grandfather how long "eventually" was, but his grandfather always said the same thing about that, too. He said that every musician was different.

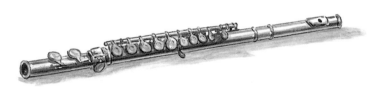

The next morning, the students in Mrs. Barry's orchestra class gathered in her classroom. They were going to have their last rehearsal in the auditorium. Daniel sat down and looked around the room. Part of one wall was covered with pictures that had been taken at all the school concerts. Daniel was in one of the pictures from the Thanksgiving concert. *But I don't*

deserve to be in it, he told himself. *Only the people who played deserve to be in that picture.* The memory of that concert six months ago still bothered him.

Then Mrs. Barry walked into the classroom. "Is everyone here?" she asked. She looked around the room and made a quick head count. "Okay, let's go." The students left the music room and headed for the auditorium. Then they walked onto the stage and sat in their assigned seats.

Daniel took his flute out of its case and sat down with the others. He looked out at the empty auditorium. Tomorrow evening it would be full. *Everyone will be here,* he thought—*Mom, Dad, Grandpa, Uncle Roger, and Aunt Libby. So will everyone else's family and friends.*

Everyone. Daniel felt his heart begin to pound and his throat start to tighten. *Cool it,* he told himself. *Just cool it.*

Mrs. Barry looked at the students, who were sitting in front of her. "This is the last rehearsal, so we'll play straight through as if it were a performance. Ready?"

The students nodded.

"Then let's begin."

Stacey was first. She picked up her violin and walked to the front of the stage. Mark was already seated at the piano. Stacey nodded, and the two began to play. At one point Mark got a little behind. Stacey slowed down, and they got back together. Mrs. Barry nodded to show her approval.

Kendra's cello solo was next. She didn't make any mistakes. Then the Sanchez twins sang a song while accompanying themselves on their guitars. They added some zippy notes at the end, and Mrs. Barry smiled.

Then it was Daniel's turn. Flute in hand, he walked to the front of the stage. He put the flute up to his mouth. Then he took a deep breath and blew—that is, he tried to blow. But no air came out of his mouth, so no notes came from the flute. He hadn't made a sound. Everyone waited. Daniel let his arms fall and then put

the flute to his mouth again. Again everyone waited patiently.

"Daniel, are you all right?" Mrs. Barry asked. She walked onto the stage to stand beside him. She bent over to talk quietly. "You know the music perfectly," she said. "Once you get the first few notes out, you'll be fine."

Daniel shook his head. "I can't."

"Never mind," Mrs. Barry said. "You can run through your piece after everyone else has finished."

That night, just like every Tuesday night, Daniel went to his grandfather's apartment. After dinner he and his grandfather sat down to play duets for piano and flute. But that night, Daniel didn't want to play.

He put his flute in his lap and told his grandfather what had happened that afternoon.

"So you rehearsed after everyone else," his grandfather said. "That's no big deal."

"You don't understand," Daniel said. "I had to rehearse in the music room because I couldn't do it on the stage. So it *is* a big deal."

"Lots of musicians have stage fright," his grandfather said for the nine-hundredth time. "I used to get stage fright myself. My knees used to shake, and my stomach did flip-flops. I still have stage fright sometimes."

"But my stage fright is worse than yours," Daniel replied. He shoved his hands in his pockets and started walking around the room. "Look, Grandpa. Whether you have stage fright or not, you get yourself on the stage, and you sit down at the piano and play. My stage fright is different. I get so scared that I can't play a single note."

"It's those first few notes," Daniel's grandfather said. "Once I play the first few notes, I'm fine. After you play the first few notes, you'll be fine, too."

Daniel plopped down in a chair. "Except I can't play the first few notes, Grandpa, so I'm NOT fine."

"Daniel, I've told you before. Lots of musicians get stage fright. Most of them get over it eventually."

"But I'm not getting over it!" Daniel's eyes filled with tears. "And I hate how I feel after I can't play. Suppose I freeze tomorrow night just like I did at the Thanksgiving concert? Suppose I can't play?"

Daniel's grandfather put his arms around him. "We all love you, Daniel. Your mother and father love you, your aunt and uncle love you, and I love you. We love you whether you play your flute or not. Remember that when you get on stage."

Grandpa's words were comforting, but they didn't help. Nothing could really help. After his grandfather walked him home, Daniel's mother asked how he was feeling. Daniel knew she was *really* asking if he would be able to play. Would he? He didn't know.

The worst part was that all the kids at school had seen him fail. They had all seen him try to play at the Thanksgiving concert and then have to leave the stage. *This is the last time,* he thought. *If I can't play this time, I'm going to quit orchestra, and I'm going to quit playing the flute. I'll give up music, and then I'll feel a lot better. I feel better already.* But he didn't feel better. He just felt sad.

CHAPTER 2
The Spring Concert

As if Daniel wasn't feeling awful enough, Zingo came over to him the next day in the cafeteria. "How's the scaredy cat?" he teased.

"Don't call me that," Daniel replied.

"Why shouldn't I? That's what you are. You're scared of playing that poor little flute. You get spooked, and you can't play. Scaredy—"

"What's going on here?" It was Mr. Kramer, the principal. Zingo headed for his seat at another table.

"Daniel, is everything all right?" asked Mr. Kramer.

"Yes, sir," Daniel answered.

"You're sure."

"I'm sure."

"We're all looking forward to the concert tonight. Good luck."

"Thank you, sir."

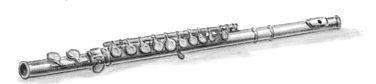

That evening Daniel tried to eat dinner, but he put down his fork after a few mouthfuls. "May I be excused?" he asked. "I'm too nervous to eat. I'd like to practice one more time."

"Of course," his mother said. "We'll all go out and have a snack after the concert, so you can eat then."

Daniel went up to his room and sat on his bed. He took his flute out of its case and stared at it. *Who am I kidding?* he wondered. *I could practice for the next hundred years, and it would never help me play.*

Soon he heard his father calling out that it was time to leave. *This has got to be the worst night of my life,* Daniel told himself. He put his flute back in the case and joined his parents in the living room. *At least I'll be back here soon, and the concert will be over,* he thought.

A half-hour later, Daniel and all the orchestra students were gathered in Mrs. Barry's classroom. As they talked among themselves, Mrs. Barry took Daniel aside. "How are you feeling?" she asked.

Daniel shook his head. "I don't know."

"Can I help?"

Daniel thought for a moment. "I'm going to try to play," he said, "but suppose I freeze? Then what?"

"How about if I give you a choice?" Mrs. Barry said.

"What do you mean?"

Mrs. Barry thought for a moment. "Here's what we'll do. When it's your turn, I'll look at you. If you want to play, nod your head. If you don't nod, we'll just go on to the next performer. Is that all right?"

"I guess," Daniel said.

"But I want you to really try to play," Mrs. Barry said firmly. Then she smiled and patted Daniel's shoulder. "You'll see. After you play tonight, it will be much easier the next time."

Daniel tried to smile back at her. He knew that playing in front of people really would be easier if he could conquer his stage fright just once. But he couldn't help thinking that she really didn't understand. Daniel picked up his flute and followed the other students to the auditorium.

It's up to me now, he thought as he walked up the stairs leading to the stage. He looked around and saw his parents and grandfather. Beside them sat his aunt and uncle.

As the students walked onto the stage, everyone in the audience began to clap. Mrs. Barry signaled for the students to sit down. Then she walked to the front of the stage and looked out at the crowd. "Welcome to our spring concert," she said. "As you can see from the program, you will hear many talented musicians and some beautiful music tonight. What you hear is the

result of many months of practice. Thank you all for
coming to honor the hard work of the Parkfield Middle
School Orchestra."

Out in the audience, Daniel's grandfather tried to
get Daniel's attention. He gave a little wave to Daniel.

"Do you think he sees us?" Daniel's mother asked
Daniel's father.

Daniel saw his family looking at him, but he didn't
smile or wave back. *I wish they hadn't come,* he thought.
I'm going to disappoint them. Still, he didn't feel as
nervous as usual. His hands weren't shaking at all.

They weren't sweaty, either. *Maybe this time I'll be okay. I won't think about anything,* he decided. *I'll just listen to the music.*

A few moments later, the concert began. Mrs. Barry introduced Stacey and Mark and the music they were about to play. Stacey walked to the front of the stage and put her violin under her chin. Then she looked over at Mark and nodded. The two began to play. *They make it look so easy,* Daniel said to himself. *They don't look nervous at all. Even when they make a mistake, they keep going as if nothing happened.*

At first the music was slow, but then the tempo picked up. Daniel saw some people in the audience nodding in time to the beat. *Everyone's having a good time,* he thought. *This is what playing is all about.* Then the audience was clapping, and Stacey and Mark were smiling and bowing.

Stacey and Mark returned to their seats, and it was Kendra's turn. She sat down and put her cello between her knees. Daniel knew she was nervous because she was biting her lower lip, but it didn't matter. The rich, full sounds came out perfectly. Soon Kendra stopped biting her lip and smiled ever so slightly.

Next the Sanchez twins sang and played their song. Daniel tried to listen, but he couldn't. He was next. If only they could sing forever so he wouldn't have to get up and play. *Stay cool*, he kept telling himself. *You can do it. Just don't think about the audience. Pretend you're playing by yourself.*

The Sanchez twins finished their song and took their bow.

Daniel felt his heart leap up into his throat. *Can I do it?* he asked himself. But the first question was whether he had the nerve to walk up to the front of the stage and try. All he could think about was the disaster at the Thanksgiving concert. *I'll freeze,* he thought. *I'm sure I will.*

Mrs. Barry was looking at Daniel, waiting for him to nod to let her know he was ready. He wanted to nod.

He wanted to play. He wanted to make his family proud of him. He looked out at his family and felt their silent message—"You can do it. You can play." He looked at the people sitting next to his family, and the people sitting next to them. The auditorium was full of people waiting impatiently.

Daniel's hands began to sweat, and fear washed over him like a blizzard hitting the Arctic. *I wish I could play,* he wanted to call out. Another moment passed, and Mrs. Barry announced the next performer. Ben stood up and walked to the front of the stage, holding his clarinet. The audience settled back and listened to its jazzy tones.

CHAPTER 3
The Picnic

The next few days were hard for Daniel, although his family had been great after the concert. His family had hugged him, and they went for ice cream as if Daniel had played and done well.

The problem was some of the other students at school, especially Zingo. During recess he always managed to get in a few "Scaredy cats." Sometimes he pretended to put a flute up to his mouth and then made a scared face. Daniel couldn't wait for the last day of school and summer vacation. Unfortunately, he still had to go to the class picnic.

Maybe our car will break down so Dad won't be able to drive us there. Better yet, maybe it will rain, he hoped. The night before the picnic, he looked up at the sky, searching for clouds. He found two little ones far away. The following morning was no better. The sun was shining in a clear blue sky.

"We have a wonderful day for the picnic," his mother said as she made sandwiches. She turned to Daniel. "Are you going to take your baseball glove?" Daniel loved to play baseball. He'd been looking forward to a good game, but now he didn't feel like it. In fact, he didn't feel like going to the picnic. All he wanted to do was stay in his room and wait for summer. "Daniel?" His mother was waiting for an answer.

"I'm not playing baseball."

Daniel's father held out his backpack. "Are you going to take your camera?" he asked. "You might want to take some pictures."

"I don't think so," Daniel said.

"Well, take it anyway," his father said. "I might want to take a shot or two."

Daniel ran up to his room and got his camera. Then he put the camera and an extra roll of film in his backpack beside his flute case. He hadn't played since the day of the rehearsal and didn't plan on ever playing again. He had even told Mrs. Barry and his parents that he was through playing music. Mrs. Barry had said, "I see." His parents had just nodded.

Daniel thought about taking the flute case out of his backpack, but his father called to him to come help load the car. Daniel zipped up the backpack and headed downstairs.

"Don't forget your jacket," his mother told him. "It might get cool later on." *Maybe it'll get freezing cold,* Daniel hoped as he grabbed his jacket. But while he loaded a huge picnic basket into the car, the sun shone even brighter. He was stuck. There was no way out.

A few moments later, Daniel and his parents got into the car and drove off. They headed toward a farm about an hour away that belonged to the school principal, Mr. Kramer. The farm lay next to a large forest. A river ran between the forest and the farm, but no one at the picnic was allowed to go in the water because it ran deep and fast.

When the Muldoons arrived, one of the fathers was organizing teams to play baseball. Mr. Muldoon looked at Daniel and pointed to the group of students. "Do you want to play?"

"No. Baseball is boring."

Daniel's mother and father looked at each other but said nothing to Daniel. "Then please give me a hand," his father said. Daniel and his father carried the picnic basket and a cooler of drinks to a spot near the river. His mother carried a blanket. "Go play and have some fun. Come back when you're hungry," she said firmly.

Daniel started to tell his mother that he wanted to go home. When he saw the look in her eyes, he decided he'd better not. He began walking slowly around the edge of the large field next to the forest. Two of his friends called out to him, but he just waved and kept

walking. The Sanchez twins were singing the song they'd sung at the spring concert. Hearing them reminded Daniel of his failure. He put his hands over his ears and sat down under a tree by the river. *I'm not going to think about that right now,* he told himself. *I'm through playing the flute. I don't care if I ever play again. I give up. I quit.*

The morning passed slowly, but finally it was lunch time, and Daniel joined his family. "Can we leave after we eat?" he asked.

"Mr. Kramer is going to take some of us on a tour of his farm," his mother replied.

"I'm not going."

"Then I'll stay with you," his mother said.

"You don't have to," Daniel said. "I brought a book. I'll sit here and read until you come back."

The Washington family was having lunch nearby, and Daniel's mother walked over to them. She spoke to them for a few moments and came back. "Mr. and Mrs. Washington will be here if you need anything," she told Daniel.

Soon after they had eaten lunch, Daniel's mother and father left with Mr. Kramer to tour the farm.

Daniel stretched out on the blanket to read, but he
didn't open his book. Instead, he closed his eyes,
enjoying the feeling of the warm sun on his face.

Then he heard a light sound. He looked up. A doe
and her fawn were running toward the river. He sat up
and watched as they drank. *I wish I had my camera!* he
thought. Then he suddenly remembered that he had
put it in his backpack. He took the camera out and put
its strap around his neck. Then he put on his backpack
so he'd have the extra roll of film.

He got up and walked slowly toward the river, trying
to focus the lens as he walked. Suddenly Zingo ran past.
"Stop!" Daniel called out. "You'll scare the deer!" But
Zingo kept on running, and the startled deer ran off
into the forest. "You scared them off!" Daniel called
out to Zingo.

Zingo trotted over to Daniel. "No, I didn't," he said.
"Why didn't you go on the tour with the others?"

"Why didn't you?" Daniel shot back.

"I wanted to explore—hey, look, they came back!" The deer were standing near the edge of the forest that dipped down to the river.

"Come on. Let's get closer," Zingo urged.

"We're not supposed to go into the forest," Daniel said.

"We're not going in the forest. We're just going to walk along the edge of the river."

"I don't think—"

"What's the matter? Are you scared of the forest like you're scared of playing your flute?"

Daniel hesitated.

"See you later, scaredy cat," Zingo said.

"Okay," Daniel said, "but this time, move slowly and be very quiet."

As the two boys followed the river, Daniel put the camera up to his eye. "Don't go any further. You'll scare them off."

"I'm just going to walk on those rocks there in the river," Zingo said.

"Be careful," Daniel said. "The rocks are wet and slippery, and you could fall in."

"So what if I do?" Zingo asked. "I know how to swim. Why don't you just stand here and watch me go?" Zingo followed the river for a short way and then walked out on a line of rocks that ran halfway across the river.

Daniel watched him for a moment and then turned his attention to the deer. They were standing quietly. Daniel raised the camera to his eye and clicked. *That is going to be a great picture,* he said to himself, *but just to make sure, I'll take another shot.* He clicked again and put the camera in his backpack. "We'd better head back," he called out to Zingo.

"Watch this!" Zingo yelled back. He lifted one leg and balanced on the other. "I'm Zingo, the famous rock hopper. Bet you can't do this, scaredy cat!"

"I'm leaving," Daniel replied and headed back the way they had come. When he heard a shout and a splash, he whirled around just in time to see Zingo being carried down the river.

Daniel froze. He took a step in one direction and then in another. Then he started running as fast as he could along the river. As he ran, he shouted, "Zingo! Zingo!" But there was no sign of Zingo.

"Zingo!" Daniel shouted again. "Where are you?"
He heard nothing. He saw nothing. Then he heard
splashing, and something came out of the water. It
was dripping. It was gasping and coughing. It was
Zingo.

CHAPTER 4

*L*ost

For a few moments, the boys rested. Then Zingo shook the water out of his shoes and pronounced himself ready to go back to the farm.

"All we have to do is follow the river," Daniel said.

"No," Zingo said. "The river twists and turns. It'll take forever that way. The best thing to do is to go straight through the forest."

"Have you ever been in the forest?"

"No."

"Then how do you expect to find your way through it?" Daniel asked.

"The farm is west of here, so all we have to do is head toward the sun."

"How do you know that?"

"My sister and I were figuring out directions when we drove here." Zingo got up and started walking. "Just trust me. I'll get us back in a jiffy."

Trusting Zingo was not exactly what Daniel wanted to do, but he didn't want to go back by himself, so he followed along.

"How did you like the way I swam and got myself out of the river?" Zingo asked, squeaking along in his wet sneakers.

"The last time I looked, you weren't exactly swimming," Daniel said.

"That's because I was resting between strokes."

Daniel shook his head and pushed some branches away from his face. "Are you sure you know where we're going?"

"Sure, I'm sure." Zingo looked up at the sky, and his face fell. "Where's the sun?"

Daniel looked up. Clouds had moved in and now covered most of the sky. Neither of them could tell where the sun was. "Let's wait and see if the clouds clear out," he suggested. He spied a fallen log to sit on and headed toward it.

"Hey!" Zingo called out. "There's a cave over there!" Zingo took off, and Daniel followed him to the mouth of a cave in the side of a rocky hill.

"This is so cool!" Zingo exclaimed. Then he began to look even more excited. "You know, I read this book about pirates. It said that some of them used to hide their treasure in caves. I'll bet there are rubies and gold and diamonds in there. I'm going to go look," he told Daniel. "Want to come?"

"No."

Zingo made a face. "Are you scared of caves, too?"

"Go explore and leave me alone," Daniel said angrily. He was sorry he had come with Zingo. *I should have just followed the river back to the farm,* he thought. *I'd probably be there by now.* Moments later, he heard shouting. He looked into the darkness. "Zingo, is that you?" he yelled.

"Help me!" Zingo answered.

"Where are you?" Daniel cried. "I don't see you."

"Face the back of the cave. Are you facing it?"

"Yes."

"Now walk slowly, one step at a time, and you'll come to a hole. I'm at the bottom of it."

Daniel thought for a second. "That doesn't sound like a good idea," he told Zingo. "What if I fall in, too?"

"Please, Daniel. You have to help me." Zingo's voice broke, and he sounded as if he were about to cry.

"Okay, I'm going to take small steps and walk very slowly. You keep talking, and I'll follow your voice."

"What do you want me to say?"

"Tell me how you got in the hole."

"Well, the ground is very soft back here. I was walking along, and the ground gave way."

"Are you all right?"

"I twisted my leg when I fell, so I can't stand on it. That's why I can't climb out."

As Daniel neared the hole, he noticed a stream of light above him. He looked up. The light was coming through a small hole in the roof of the cave. Daniel looked down to see Zingo sitting at the bottom of a very deep hole.

CHAPTER 5

Time to Play

"How can one person get into so much trouble?" Daniel asked.

"I always look for adventure," Zingo said. "*Danger is my middle name. Unlike you, I have courage.*"

"Well, okay, Mr. Courage, you make yourself comfortable in the hole. I have to get going."

"What?" Zingo sounded panicky.

"I said I have to get going."

"You're going to leave me here?"

"Zingo, you're stuck in that hole. You can't get out and I can't get you out. I'm going to get some help."

"No! You're not going anywhere. You're not going to leave me here all alone!"

"What can happen? It's not like we're in a really dangerous place, like a jungle. This is Connecticut."

A moment of silence followed.

"Zingo?" Daniel called.

"Look, I didn't want to tell you this before because I didn't want to scare you, but I'm pretty sure there's a wild creature living in this cave."

"How do you know that?"

"Right after I fell in the hole I heard some weird noises—animal noises."

"I don't hear anything."

"Daniel, I'm telling you I heard them, so that means it's here in the cave with us."

"Fine. You heard a wild animal. That doesn't mean it's going to come down in the hole and get you."

"We don't know that, do we? What if it's hungry? Suppose it like holes. Suppose it likes THIS hole. Then what?"

"Zingo, this is really dumb. I have to go get help."

"You don't know how to get back to the farm. We're lost, remember?"

"I'll go back to the river and follow it. That's what we should have done in the first place. You take it easy, and I'll be back as soon as I can."

"Daniel, I know I shouldn't be asking you, but please, oh, please, don't leave me. Just stay here with me. Somebody will find us. Daniel?"

"What?"

"Daniel, I know I said Danger is my middle name, and all that, but here's the thing." He stopped talking.

Daniel waited.

"I don't want you to leave me because I'm . . ."

"You're what? I know you're scared of something, so just say it."

"I'm scared of the dark."

So the one who called me scaredy cat is afraid of the dark, Daniel thought, but he didn't say anything. He knew how he had felt when Zingo made fun of his fear.

Daniel was quiet for a long moment. "Okay. I'll stay with you. But now we have to figure out a way to get some help." He looked at his watch. "It's almost four, so everybody's getting ready to leave. That means they'll notice we're not there and start looking for us.

The problem is that this is a pretty big forest. We need to figure out how to let them know where we are."

"We could build a big fire," Zingo offered.

"Right. Except we don't have any matches, and I'm not very good at rubbing sticks together."

"We could make a lot of noise."

"You can't make much noise from inside that hole, and my voice isn't going to carry very far."

"I wish I had my special dog whistle with me," Zingo said.

"What's that?"

"It has a very high sound. People can't hear it, but dogs can."

"That's a cool thing to have but—"

Zingo interrupted him. "Look in your pockets. Maybe you have something that will make a loud noise."

"Right. I always carry a spare car horn when I go to a picnic."

"Look anyway," Zingo said.

Daniel put his hands into his empty pockets.

"Daniel?"

"Yeah?"

"Nothing. I was just making sure you're still here."

"I won't leave," Daniel said. "I'm just thinking."

"Did you check your pockets?"

"Yeah. They're empty."

"What about your backpack?"

"Zingo, you're driving me crazy."

"Just check it."

Daniel reached for his backpack, unzipped it, and looked inside. "I've got my camera and my flute." He sat down and pulled his knees up under his chin. *There must be something I can do, but what? Use what you have,* he thought. *So what do I have besides my camera and my flute? Wait a minute! I have my flute! That's it!*

"Zingo!" he yelled. "I can play my flute. I'll stand outside the cave, and I'll play as loudly as I can. Someone's bound to hear it."

"Great," Zingo said. "But promise just to stand outside the cave. Don't leave."

"I promise." Daniel walked outside. The sky was still light, but the forest was growing dark. He listened for voices, but he heard none. He took his flute out of its case and put it to his lips. He thought about Zingo listening to him play, and his throat tightened. *This is important,* he told himself. *I need to let everyone know where we are.* He took a deep breath and tried to blow. Nothing.

This is no time for stage fright, he told himself. *It's time for facing my music and my fear.* He took another deep breath and tried to blow again. Again nothing. *I am NOT a scaredy cat. I CAN play. I WILL play!*

For the third time, Daniel took a deep breath. This time, the air flew into his flute. A trio of notes burst out and then another and another, and then Daniel played the song he had prepared for the spring concert. The notes—round, full, and rich—flew out over the trees and lingered in the air.

"Did you hear that?"

"It sounded like a flute."

"That was wonderful!"

"What beautiful music!"

The voices came out of the forest. They belonged to his mother and father, Zingo's parents, and everybody else's parents, too.

Daniel sighed with relief. As his mother and father hugged him, the giant weight of his fear slipped from him. While Zingo's parents and others rescued Zingo from the hole, Daniel looked down and noticed how his flute reflected the last of the daylight in the forest. For the first time in a very long time, he saw how bright his flute was, and how its brightness lit up the world around him.